Wolf on the l

By Sally Pfou
Illustrated by Doris Weeks

Doris Weeks and Sally Pfoutz created this book out of a love of all living creatures and dedicate it to children everywhere. Please always do whatever you can to protect and cherish the beauty of the earth and all of its creatures.

Doris Weeks

When the wolf is on the run swans sound the alarm.

Trumpeter Swans

When the wolf is on the run the heron takes flight.

Great Blue Heron

When the wolf is on the run pelicans hit the water.

American White Pelicans

When the wolf is on the run the owl keeps watch.

Snowy Owl

The wolf is on the run.

When she was small Nikita never worried. As long as her mother was by her side, she felt safe and happy.

When she grew up and went out on her own, she still wasn't afraid, but she was lonely. So she ran forty miles in all directions, exploring, looking for friends, and searching for a mate. She was heading west when she picked up a scent.

She turned around and headed east.

She ran up the mountain. She ran down the mountain. She got to running so fast she couldn't stop. She tumbled around all topsy-turvy. She was running in thin air for a moment or two and she appeared to be running upside-down.

A pair of peregrine falcons thought the young wolf was behaving quite strangely.

Kestrels took to the trees.

The whooping crane was preening and didn't notice.

Sandhill cranes
flew to the edge.

Great blue herons stayed put.

Nikita went for a swim as the moon rose in the sky.

Soon she was on the run again.

Nighttime fell and the sky was the color of midnight.

The next morning, Nikita watched from a distance as two other wolves chased an elk, leaping and bounding through the snow.

A rough-legged hawk kept an eye on the wolves.

The wolves scattered as they heard explosions and smelled danger.
Crows flew along with Nikita as if to show her the way to safety.

When she finally stopped, the raven flew down to her side and asked: What is it, child?

It is me. I do not want to be a wolf.

Why ever not? I have always admired the wolf. Wolves are unafraid, strong, fast, skillful, and clever. Your mother Veruschka was swift and proud, with a coat so thick and soft you could bury yourself in her side and never want to come out.

I remember.

Your father was fearless and reckless. When he appeared, birds flew to the treetops, mice burrowed under, deer froze. Even elk sometimes twice his size ran because their very lives depended on it.

I did not hear it; I saw it every time people looked fearful and pointed guns and arrows at me, every time rabbits and other creatures ran away. I could not make one friend out there and that is because wolves are mean.

Suddenly the bird flapped his wings and sailed straight up into the sky. Nikita saw a shadow from the corner of her eye and the sweet scent of wolf twirled about her head and settled on her face. She could taste it on her lips. Her nose twitched and her shoulders quivered.

She leapt up, spun around, and hunched down, snarling. But it was only old black wolf, so close, Nikita could feel his hot breath and see herself in his glinty eyes.

Old black wolf sniffed and walked on by. He looked way off into the distance and said: Wolves are not mean, child. They are wild.

Yes, even savage. Eating what they kill. For wolves, this is natural.

Wolves are heroic. When the glaciers rolled in and broke away the land, many suffered and died, but not the wolves.

When humans came and took everything—the tall trees, the miles of mountain, the free-flowing rivers—wolves stayed and tried to survive.

When humans went out like soldiers and killed every wolf they saw, there were still some that got away.

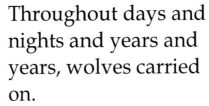

Throughout days and nights and years and years, wolves carried on.

No, wolves are not mean, child, they are wild; gentle with their pups, playful with their pack.

They take care of each other; hunt together, sing at dusk.

Old black wolf raised his nose to the wind. His mouth dropped open and he called out to the pink and yellow sky, to the sinking sun.

Hello, I am the wolf. I belong in the wilderness. Please do not take it away. Do not take me away. For I am the wolf; not mean, child, only wild.

Made in the USA
Middletown, DE
28 October 2017